Children of Long Ago

poems by **Lessie Jones Little**

pictures by **Jan Spivey Gilchrist**

introduction by **Eloise Greenfield**

LEE & LOW BOOKS Inc.
New York

With love, to all my family, past and present
                                       —L.J.L.

For Mama, Daddy, Kelvin, Ronké, and William.
Thanks to Lakeshia and Tamica and especially to
Eloise Greenfield who believed I could paint her
mother's beautiful words   —J.S.G.

"Mama's Grandpa Clock" previously published in *Ebony, Jr.*, December, 1984

Printed in Hong Kong by South China Printing Co. (1988) Ltd.

Book design by Tania Garcia
Book production by The Kids at Our House

The text is set in Bembo
The illustrations are rendered in pastel

10 9 8 7 6 5 4 3 2 1
First LEE & LOW Edition, 2000

Library of Congress Cataloging-in-Publication Data
Little, Lessie Jones.
    Children of long ago : poems / by Lessie Jones Little ; pictures by Jan
Spivey Gilchrist ; introduction by Eloise Greenfield.— 1st Lee & Low ed.
      p. cm.
    Summary: A collection of seventeen poems that detail the daily pleasures
of the African American childhood during the early 1900s.
    ISBN 1-58430-008-6
    1. Afro-Americans—Juvenile poetry. 2. Children's poetry, American—
Afro-American authors. [1. Afro-Americans—Poetry. 2. American poetry—
Afro-American authors.] I. Gilchrist, Jan Spivey, ill. II. Title.
PS3562.I78288 C5 2000
811'.54—dc21   99-056100

Lessie Jones Little, the author of *Children of Long Ago,* was my mother. In this book, she has mixed her memories and her imagination to create children growing up during the time of her childhood, the early 1900s. Life was quite different then. There were almost no planes, very few cars, and no television.

The book is about happy times, although not all of my mother's childhood experiences were happy. Sometimes there was no food, and she was hungry. Once, for about two years, her parents were separated, and some of her days were sad. But most of her memories were good ones. When I was a child, I enjoyed hearing my mother and her sisters laughing and talking about the funny things they had seen and done when they were children.

My mother didn't live to see the art for *Children of Long Ago,* but I know how she would have felt about it. She loved beautiful art. Sometimes she would slide her fingers very gently across the page of a book, as if she were actually touching the face, or sky, or river that the artist had painted.

I am grateful that my mother was my mother. As I write this, I am sad, missing her. But I am also joyful because she still lives in the hearts of many who knew her and in the words she has left for all of us. With her poems, she makes us laugh and think and learn. She takes us back in time and lets us see and hear and enjoy getting to know the life she knew so long ago.

Eloise Greenfield

Children of Long Ago

The children who lived a long time ago
In little country towns
Ate picnics under spreading trees,
Played hopscotch on the cool dirt yards,
Picked juicy grapes from broad grapevines,
Pulled beets and potatoes from the ground,
Those children of long ago.

The children who lived a long time ago
In little country towns
Tromped to school on hard-frozen roads,
Warmed themselves by wood-burning stoves,
Ate supper by light from oil-filled lamps,
Built fancy snowmen dressed like clowns,
Those children of long ago.

The children who lived a long time ago
In little country towns
Decked themselves in their Sunday best,
Went to church and visited friends,
Sang happy songs with their mamas and papas,
Traveled through books for sights and sounds,
Those children of long ago.

All Dressed Up

The church bell is ringing bong-bong, bong-bong.
It sounds like it's saying, "Come along, come along."

The folks are wearing their best Sunday clothes,
Miss Lossie in her seamed-back hose,
Mr. George in a straw hat with a black band,
Miss Lou carrying a big fancy fan,

Emmett in knee-pants and long black stockings,
Rubber-soled shoes for easy walking,
Little Lucy in a long-waisted, pleated dress,
With rickrack braid across the chest.

The townsfolk dress up in their nicest things
And strut to church when the church bell rings.

Bells

Ricky rings the bell in the school yard,
    He pulls the rope hard.

Dinner is ready, Mama rings the bell,
    All is well.

The cowbells are ringing, the cows are coming home,
    The day is done.

Papa rings the church bell in the steeple
    To call the people.

Reading Glasses

Read me a story, Grandma, please,
About doggies and kitties and trips and trees,
About chickens in the yard and children in the house,
About a plowing horse and a little field mouse,
About frisky snowflakes romping above
And mamas and papas and joy and love.

Your eyeglasses are pretty and thin and clear
With long gold arms that hug your ears.
They hold on to your face and never fall
And when I grow up to be big and tall,
I'll buy me some reading eyeglasses, too,
And they'll make me read just like you.

Wait Little Joe

"That ditch is too wide," I told Little Joe.
"Thomas is ten, you're only four, you know."

"I can jump that ditch," said Little Joe,
So he pitched himself as far as he could go,
But he missed the mark and landed in the middle!
And he knew at once that he was too little.

Bill fished him out and made him promise
That he wouldn't jump again till he was big as Thomas.

Paper Dolls

Bring your children for a dinner treat,
We'll make a cardboard table where they can eat.
We'll have a place for them to sit
In cardboard chairs that they can fit.

We'll pick blackberries for their meal,
But we'll eat their meal since they're not real.
We cut them from books with scissors small,
You see, they're not real children at all.
They're only paper dolls.

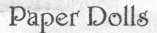

Papa's Cutting Wood

Papa lifts his arms,
Swings the sharp ax,
Brings it down to the wood with a hard whack.
His muscles balloon,
His breath blows a tune,
Papa's cutting wood on the woodpile.

The ax strikes the wood
With a loud crack,
The sharp blow shakes Papa's arms and back,
The wood pops a sound,
Falls to the ground,
Papa's cutting wood on the woodpile.

Papa's getting tired, but he cuts till dark,
Enough for the bedroom and the kitchen woodbox,
Papa's cutting wood on the woodpile.

The Woodbox

Mr. Empty Woodbox,
Sitting idly by,
How can Mama make a meal
When there's no wood for fire?

Mr. Empty Woodbox,
I know what to do,
I'll bring wood from the woodpile
And dump it all in you.

Mama's Grandpa Clock

I like my mama's grandpa clock
Standing tall against the wall.
It speaks to me all through the day
With its ringing, bong–bong call.

In the morning when its hands move 'round
To make a wide open V,
It rings eight bong–bongs and I know
My papa's leaving me.

It's time for lunch, it's time to nap,
As I snuggle under the cover.
It's time to go outside and play
When napping time is over.

When the hands on its silver face stretch out
Toward the ceiling and toward the floor,
And its bong–bong sings out six loud rings,
My papa's at the door.

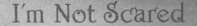

I'm Not Scared

Can I play with Emma Lee?
She's my dearest friend.
Emma Lee lives down the road
Around the railroad bend.

Can I go to Emma Lee's?
Those train cars standing there
Don't have an engine fastened on,
They can't move anywhere.

Cows are grazing in the street
As far as I can see.
They're much bigger than I am,
Their sharp horns point at me.

But I'm not scared of all those cows,
They're just eating grass.
They'll lift their heads and stare at me,
I'll just walk right past.

Can I go to Emma Lee's?
We'll jump and skip and run.
I can go all by myself,
I'll come back by one.

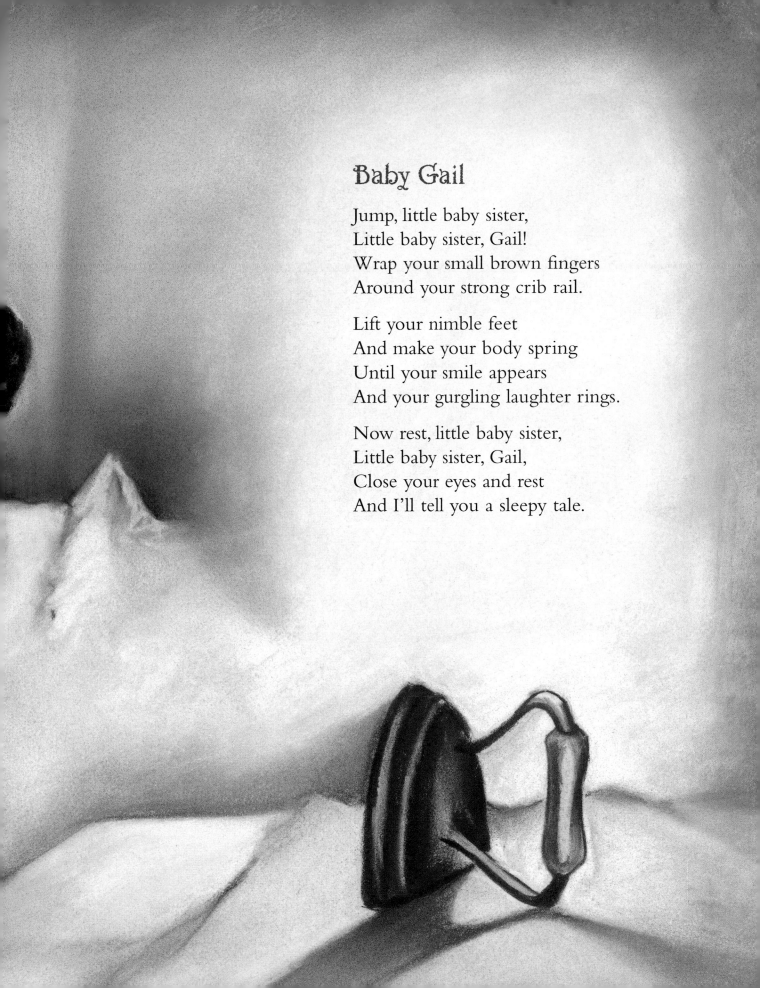

Baby Gail

Jump, little baby sister,
Little baby sister, Gail!
Wrap your small brown fingers
Around your strong crib rail.

Lift your nimble feet
And make your body spring
Until your smile appears
And your gurgling laughter rings.

Now rest, little baby sister,
Little baby sister, Gail,
Close your eyes and rest
And I'll tell you a sleepy tale.

Let's Go Barefoot

Let's take off our shoes and go barefoot.
    The sun is warm,
    The air is mild,
For just a little while, let's go barefoot.

Let's put our feet in the soft, cool dirt.
    It rained last night,
    The earth is damp,
Let's run down the ramp and walk barefoot.

Cornfield Leaves

Silky ribbons long and green,
Dotted with sparkling dew,
Waving in the summer breeze
Under a roof of blue.

Keep on waving in the breeze,
Keep on sparkling, too,
And every time you wave at me,
I'll wave right back at you.

My Black Hen

I love Sue, my sleek black hen,
I know she loves me, too.
Sis Carrie feeds the other chicks
But I feed only Sue.

She comes and stands in the backyard
Close beside my feet.
I throw out grains of yellow corn
Just for my Sue to eat.

When she has finished eating corn,
And I talk as I stoop down,
Her round eyes blink, she's not afraid,
She chatters with a clucky sound.

Going to Sunday School

Trot good old big horse rusty red,
We're going to learn the golden rule.
Stir up the dust in the long dirt road,
We're on our way to Sunday school.

Papa says, "Giddap," and away we go.
The buggy is rocking from side to side,
I'm bobbing and bumping on Mama's lap,
We're taking our bouncy buggy ride.

The four big wheels are spinning around,
The wind in our faces is calm and cool,
A little while longer and we'll be there,
We're on our way to Sunday school.

My Yellow Straw Hat

Wearing my yellow straw hat
(Mama had just bought it),
I was going to see Aunt Bett
When a high wind caught it,

Took it up in the air
As I cried and watched it
Sailing high up there
Where I couldn't catch it,

Dropped it down in the ditch
Where the water snatched it,
Made it tumble and pitch
Till the wetness had stretched it.

It was soggy and wet
When my aunt Bett found it.
She dried my yellow hat
And put a new ribbon 'round it.

Children of Long Ago

Sometimes sad and sorry,
Sometimes jolly and glad,
    They cried,
    They laughed,
    They worked,
    They played,
    They learned,
    They loved,
Those children of long ago.